Speedsters...

The Seven-and-one-half Labors of HERCULES

by John Bendall-Brunello

DUTTON CHILDREN'S BOOKS

NEW YORK

Dedicated to
my wife
TIZIANA
for all her helpful
suggestions & support

Speedsters is a trademark of Dutton Children's Books.

Library of Congress Cataloging-in-Publication Data

Bendall-Brunello, John.
  The seven-and-one-half labors of Hercules / by John Bendall-
Brunello.—1st ed.
    p. cm.
  Summary: A young boy tackles a list of chores with disastrous
results.
  ISBN 0-525-44780-6
  [1. Work—Fiction. 2. Humorous stories.] I. Title. II. Title:
7½ labors of Hercules.
PZ7.B43135Se 1991
[Fic]—dc20   91-36176
                                                         CIP
                                                          AC

Published in the United States by Dutton Children's Books,
a division of Penguin Books USA Inc.
375 Hudson Street, New York, New York 10014

Printed in U.S.A.   First Edition
10 9 8 7 6 5 4 3 2 1

How it all began...

This is a story about a boy named Hercules. You probably don't know anyone named Hercules. But you may have heard the name before.

Once, a long time ago, there was a man named Hercules who was very strong. He performed many difficult tasks and became a famous hero.

The Hercules in this story is not a hero. He is an ordinary kid, with a not-so-ordinary name.

One morning Hercules got up very late.
In fact, it was so late that he missed
breakfast with his parents. They were
gone when he got downstairs.

Instead he found a note on the table. It
was stuck under Grandma's broken flower
vase. Hercules pulled the note out. It was
a list of things to do.

To Do

1. Water the garden.
2. Pick apples from Mrs. Dragon's orchard.
3. Fix Grandma's vase.
4. Get the birds out of the garden. (They're eating the vegetables again.)
5. Clean the stairs.
6. Take the neighbor's dog for a walk.
7. Pay the milk bill.

P. S.

Hercules read the list. It looked like a lot of work, but he thought he could do it.

I'm not named Hercules for nothing.

The First Labor

The first item on the list said:

1. Water the garden.

So Hercules went out to the shed and found the big watering can.

He filled it up from the garden tap.

Then he carried the heavy can to the garden.

So Hercules found the hose. He attached it to the tap.

Then he turned on the water all the
way. But a few seconds later, he wished
he hadn't.

First the hose began to wiggle.

Then it writhed like a huge snake.

It jumped and jittered.

Somehow it managed to wrap itself
around Hercules and lift him in the air.

Then water shot out of the hose full force.
It blasted the plants and flattened the
flowers and flooded the garden.

The water was pouring out so fast that it snapped the hose right off the tap! Suddenly the whole thing gave a shudder, and Hercules fell down

right into a great big puddle.

Hercules had water in his ears,

water in his eyes,

and water in his boots.

The Second Labor

Hercules was still wet when he checked the list for the next job.

2. Pick apples from Mrs. Dragon's orchard.

Hercules went across the road into Mrs. Dragon's orchard. He began to pick apples and put them, one by one, into a wheelbarrow he found next to a tree.

He grabbed the wheelbarrow and ran as
fast as he could toward one of the trees.

BANG!

The apples rained down into the wheelbarrow. He went to the next tree.

BANG!

More apples came down.

BANG!

Hercules was so excited that he didn't notice Mrs. Dragon standing right in his way. By accident, he pushed the wheelbarrow straight into her legs.

Down went Mrs. Dragon. Out fell the
apples, all over her.

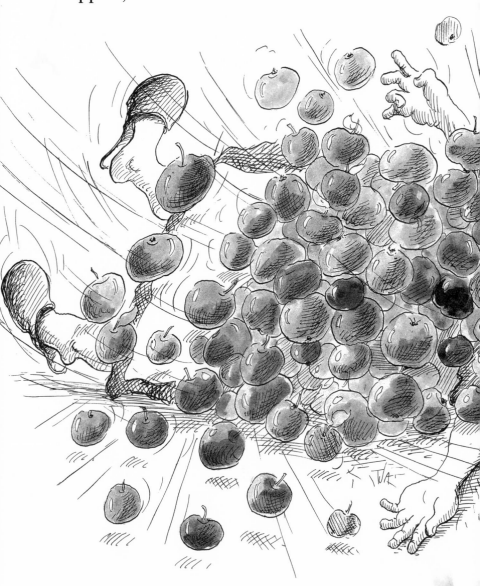

The next minute her red face popped
out of the pile of apples.

You
there !
Come back
here !

Hercules looked back at her. Then he
ran home as fast as he could, without
stopping for any apples at all.

17

The Third Labor

When Hercules got home, he sat down at the kitchen table to rest. There he saw the note again. The next item said:

3. Fix Grandma's vase.

Hercules stuffed the note into his pocket. Then he examined the vase. It was broken in several places.

He got the glue and brought it to the table.

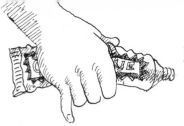

He squeezed the tube,
but nothing came out.

He gave the glue another squeeze. Still
nothing came out.

Then he gave it a *really* hard squeeze.

The glue finally came out—all over
Hercules and everything else.

In a panic he reached for a towel to wipe his hands. They were so full of glue they stuck to a plate on the table instead.

He tried to push the plate off his hand
with a spoon. But that stuck too.

Things got worse.

He stuck to a knife, two forks,

and some pieces of Grandma's vase.

The glue was beginning to dry. So he
quickly joined all the things on his hands
together to make . . .

one big vase!

It looked a bit different.

The Fourth Labor

Hercules was still peeling the glue off his hands as he took the list out of his pocket to see what was next.

4. Get the birds out of the garden.

Hercules went outside. A large blackbird was pecking at the sweet corn, calmly pulling off great big pieces.

Another bird flew down and began to do the same thing. Hercules shouted at them, but they just ignored him.

More blackbirds joined the others. Hercules tried clapping his hands *and* shouting. The birds all ignored Hercules.

Next, he tried throwing big globs of
mud at the birds. But they weren't
frightened at all.

Hercules ran inside and started pulling things out of a big box in the hall.

When he was ready, he crept back
outside. He wanted to catch the birds by
surprise.

There they were, the greedy things.
Hercules jumped up and—

The birds flew off in every direction.

In his excitement Hercules had trampled down all the sweet corn in the garden. He had done more damage than the birds!

So he decided to get on with the next job . . . quickly.

The Fifth Labor

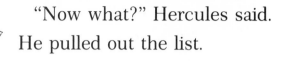

"Now what?" Hercules said.
He pulled out the list.

5. Clean the stairs.

Hercules decided to give them a quick
once-over with the vacuum cleaner.

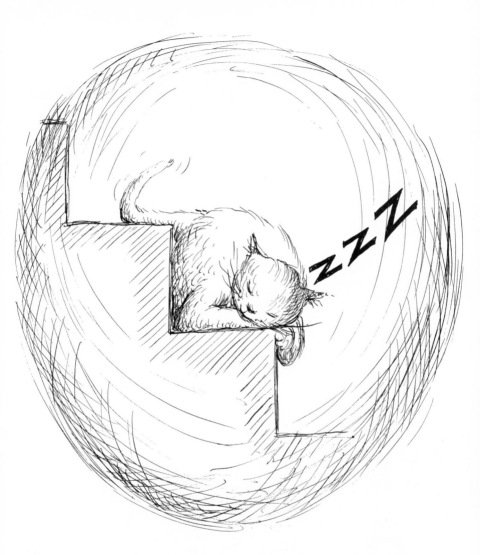

He started at the top and zoomed down,
sucking up all the dirt and dust. In his
hurry he didn't notice the family cat,
Snowball, fast asleep on the stairs.

All of a sudden there was a

followed by a

and a very loud

Oh no! I've sucked the cat into the vacuum cleaner!

As Hercules bent down to turn off the
machine, it pitched forward.

The vacuum cleaner, Hercules, and
Snowball the cat banged down the stairs.

As it landed with a thud, the vacuum
cleaner broke open, sending out a great
cloud of dust.

The stairs and the hall were covered
with dust.

The vacuum cleaner was broken.

Snowball was the color of mud.

But Snowball had had enough for one
day. She ran off.

Hercules decided to leave the cleaning
and get on with his next job.

The Sixth Labor

The next job on the list said:

6. Take the neighbor's dog for a walk.

That dog? UH-OH!

The neighbor's dog was enormous. It had huge teeth and a horrible growl.

He'll take ME for a walk!

Hercules went next door. The dog was asleep on the porch. Its leash was lying nearby.

Hercules tiptoed up to the porch

one

step

at

a

time.

He slowly picked up the leash. The dog didn't seem to notice him.

Hercules carefully slipped the leash on the dog. It didn't even growl.

Just as Hercules thought everything was all right, the dog bounded off, pulling Hercules behind him.

They tore along the street.

Ahead, three old ladies were waiting at the bus stop, directly in their path. The dog kept right on going.

BAM!

The old ladies
scattered
in all directions.

A man stood behind them with his
shopping cart full of groceries.

What a mess!

Next, the dog raced into Mr. Sticks'
bakery, pulling Hercules behind him.

Tray after tray of cakes and pies and
cookies and breads were knocked to the
floor.

Suddenly the dog stopped. He began to sniff Mr. Sticks. Then he jumped on the baker, knocked him down, and began to lick his face.

Hercules crept out of the shop, hoping Mr. Sticks wouldn't come after him. But he didn't need to worry. The dog was still sitting on Mr. Sticks, licking his face.

The Seventh Labor

Hercules checked the list
to see what was next.

7. Pay the milk bill.

The dairy was kind of far away, so
Hercules stopped at home to get his bike.
Then he set off to the dairy farm to pay
the farmer.

When he reached the farm gate, he got off his bike, opened the gate, and carefully closed it behind him.

Just as he was getting back on his bike again, he saw the huge bull owned by the farmer. The bull saw him too.

Suddenly, the bull started toward him with its head down. Hercules began to pedal as hard as he could. He kept turning his head to look behind him.

So Hercules didn't see the huge
haystack looming in front of him!
Suddenly the bull butted him

BANG!

onto the top of the haystack.

The bull went on, charging straight
through the haystack and into the fence.
His horns stuck tight.

SPLASH!

Hercules began to laugh. He laughed so hard he slipped down the other side of the haystack and into the water trough.

Hercules stopped laughing just in time to look up at the farmer. He had come to see what the ruckus was about. The farmer burst into laughter.

The farmer put Hercules into the
tractor and gave him a bumpy ride home.

P. S.

As Hercules wheeled his bike up the driveway, he took another look at the list. At the bottom, right where the note was torn, it said:

But before Hercules could figure it out, he came to his front door.

There was a surprise in store for him.

Waiting in a long line were:
1. Dad with some very wet-looking plants.
2. Mrs. Dragon with a basket of apples.
3. Grandma with her vase.
4. Mom with the instruments.
5. Snowball the cat, perched on the broken vacuum cleaner.

6. The three old ladies from the bus
   stop and the man with some torn
   shopping bags and Mr. Sticks with
   the neighbor's dog.

Everybody was looking at Hercules in a
strange way. No one looked very happy.

"Hercules, what have you been up to?" asked his mother.

Hercules looked at all the angry people. "I tried to do the things on the list," he said. "But they were too hard."

"I'm sorry," Hercules mumbled. "The real Hercules wouldn't have made such a mess of things."

After Hercules told everyone he was sorry, they all got together to help clean up. With so many people working, it was the easiest job of all.

"Gosh," said Hercules, "I wish you had been here to help me before! I've done everything except the *P.S.* But I don't know what it was. It got ripped off the note."

"Here it is!" called his grandmother. "It's stuck to my vase! It says . . ."

"Oh," said Hercules. "I'll save that one for tomorrow. I wonder what other jobs I can find."